DISCARD

.

Feraj and the Magic Lute

AN ARABIAN FOLKTALE

Retold by Ann Malaspina • Illustrated by Martina Peluso

Published by The Child's World®
1980 Lookout Drive • Mankato, MN 56003-1705
800-599-READ • www.childsworld.com

Acknowledgments
The Child's World®: Mary Berendes, Publishing Director
Red Line Editorial: Editorial direction and production
The Design Lab: Design

ISBN 978-1623236137
LCCN 2013931378

Printed in the United States of America
Mankato, MN
July, 2013
PA02167

 eraj was a man who had never learned a trade. He wandered from place to place. He never stayed anywhere for long. Sometimes he stole milk from a shepherd's goat or took eggs from a chicken. When night fell, he slept on the hard ground.

One morning, Feraj came to the house of the wealthiest man in the valley. Standing at the gate, he stared in amazement. Not long ago, the rich man had ridden an old donkey and begged for his supper. Now the man had many servants. He had a grove of orange trees. He also had his own elephant to take him where he pleased.

Feraj noticed a small lute under a tree in the garden. His grandfather used to tell stories about a magic lute that brought great wealth to its owner. Feraj stared at the instrument. No wonder its owner now rode an elephant instead of a donkey!

After dark, Feraj snuck into the garden. He wrapped the lute in his robe and hurried away. He ran and ran, out into the desert. Soon the lights of the village had faded behind him. Feraj stopped to look at his treasure.

In his hands, the small instrument looked very plain. Feraj plucked a string, but the note was out of tune. No riches appeared. Disappointed, Feraj fell asleep on the sand. As the moon moved across the sky, a sweet song filled the starry night.

Silk and jewels. Incense and myrrh.
This magic lute brings wealth to
the poor.
If you listen and do not sleep,
A bag of gold will be yours to keep.

The lute sang all night long. But Feraj slept deeply. He had forgotten the most important part of his grandfather's story.

Only those who hear the lute's night song will be rewarded, his grandfather had said.

Days passed. Feraj made his way from place to place. He stole food along the way, but he never stayed anywhere for long. The lute was silent all day. At night its song began again, but Feraj was never awake to hear it.

At the edge of the desert, Feraj met a young man. The young man complained that his pockets were empty. He could not buy figs and pistachios for his mother, who waited at home.

Feraj thought of a way the lute could finally do him some good. "I'll make you a bargain," Feraj told the young man. He held out the lute. "I will give you this magic lute. In return, you will give me your house."

The young man looked at the instrument. "Why would I make such a terrible bargain?"

"This magic lute will bring you great wealth," Feraj said. "Your mother will never be hungry again."

It sounded too good to be true. But the young man was desperate. He took the lute from Feraj. "I hope you are not lying to me," he said.

Feraj nodded, pretending to be sincere. He was tired of wandering. He wanted a roof over his head. And it did not matter to Feraj if he had to cheat someone else to get it.

Feraj followed the young man up a dusty path. The mother waited outside a little cottage. "Where are the figs and pistachios?" she asked her son.

"I brought you something much finer," said the young man, handing her the instrument. "This magic lute will bring us great wealth."

When he explained his bargain with Feraj, the mother's face turned red in anger. "Foolish boy!" she cried. "You've been tricked, and now we have nothing."

She and her son had no choice but to leave the cottage to Feraj. Since they had no home, they put up a tent in the desert. The tent did not keep out the cold night wind. The mother was able to fall asleep, but the young man tossed and turned in the chilly air. Then, as the moon moved across the sky, he heard a sweet song. It was coming from the lute!

Silk and jewels. Incense and myrrh.
This magic lute brings wealth to
the poor.
If you listen and do not sleep,
A bag of gold will be yours to keep.

The young man picked up the lute excitedly. He found a bag of gold under it, sinking in the sand. The tired young man fell asleep clutching the bag. In the morning, he showed his mother the gold. He told her what he remembered of the lute's song. But because he was so tired, he forgot the last two lines.

His mother placed the lute in the sand. She stared at it, waiting for gold to appear. She shook and hit the lute. But another bag did not appear. She convinced her son that the gold must have come to them in a dream. She forgave him for being foolish, and they went shopping in the bazaar. With the gold they bought nuts, fruit, and many expensive new clothes. But they still had no home.

One day, the king's vizier saw them in the square. As the adviser to the king, he was very sharp. The vizier noticed the mother and son's new leather sandals and silk robes trimmed with fur. They looked so noble that the vizier invited them to work for the king, helping to oversee his

land. There, every meal was a feast, and the mother and son had no worries at all.

They were so content that the young man soon forgot all about the message in the lute's song. He slept well every night and never heard it again. Every so often, his mother would shake the lute just in case it was indeed magical. She would knock it against the floor, hoping that a bag of gold would fall out. But it never did.

One day, the young man came across a new hire scrubbing dirty pots in the king's kitchen. He recognized him at once. It was Feraj!

"What are you doing here?" the young man asked.

Feraj explained that he had left rice boiling on the fire during an afternoon nap. The cottage burned to the ground, and he lost everything. Having outgrown his old lifestyle, Feraj had no choice but to come clean for the king for food and shelter.

The mother took pity on Feraj and let him sleep on their rug at night. She was no longer angry about the bargain her son had made. Since both the young man and his mother now believed the lute was worthless, they gave it back to Feraj.

After long days spent washing dirty pots, Feraj slept deeply every night. With no one listening, the lute kept its secret for many years.

21

Arabic-Speaking Countries

Asia

Africa

FOLKTALES

Long ago, Arabian folktales were told in the deserts of North Africa, in the bazaars of Damascus in Syria, and on the hills of Jerusalem. These stories were passed along from old to young for generations. They reflected the culture of the Arabian people, who originally inhabited the Arabian Peninsula, North Africa, and the Middle East.

Arabian people are made up of many ethnic groups and religions. But many Arabs share similar beliefs and traditions. Storytelling is one such tradition. Arabian tales are full of humor, tragedy, love, and revenge. Many follow the adventures of powerful sultans and poor cobblers. Some are tales of jealous siblings and tragic princesses, or spirits with magical powers. Some Arabian stories teach lessons. Others are fun and entertaining.

Many folktales were told orally, or by speaking, before being written down. There are often many versions of these stories. The story that you just read about Feraj and the magic lute is based on a written version by Jean Russell Larson. Larson's version was published in 1971 in the book *The Glass Mountain and Other Arabian Tales.*

The lute in the story is an ancient stringed instrument. It has been played by Arabic people since the seventh century. It is called the *oud*, or *ud*, in Arabic-speaking countries. The lute's sound is sweet and haunting. The magical lute in the story also sings. But although its owners want the lute to make them rich, they never seem to listen to it or remember its message. Why do you think that is?

ABOUT THE ILLUSTRATOR

Martina Peluso is an Italian illustrator represented by Advocate Art Illustration Agency. Martina lives in Naples, Italy, with her two cats, Peppe and Ernesto, and she would like to widen her family with a goose, a dog, and a donkey, all living in her little house.

Peluso has exhibited her work at many different shows all over the world, such as the International Academy of Illustration in Torino, Italy. Nowadays, Peluso spends her time mainly concentrating on children's illustration.